London

ST PAUL'S CATHEDRAL

The TOWER of London

BLACKFRIARS BRIDGE

MILLENNIUM BRIDGE

SOUTHWARK BRIDGE

LONDON BRIDGE

RIVER THAMES

TATE MODERN

GLOBE THEATRE

This book belongs to . . .

TOWER BRIDGE

Mr Chicken lands on LONDON

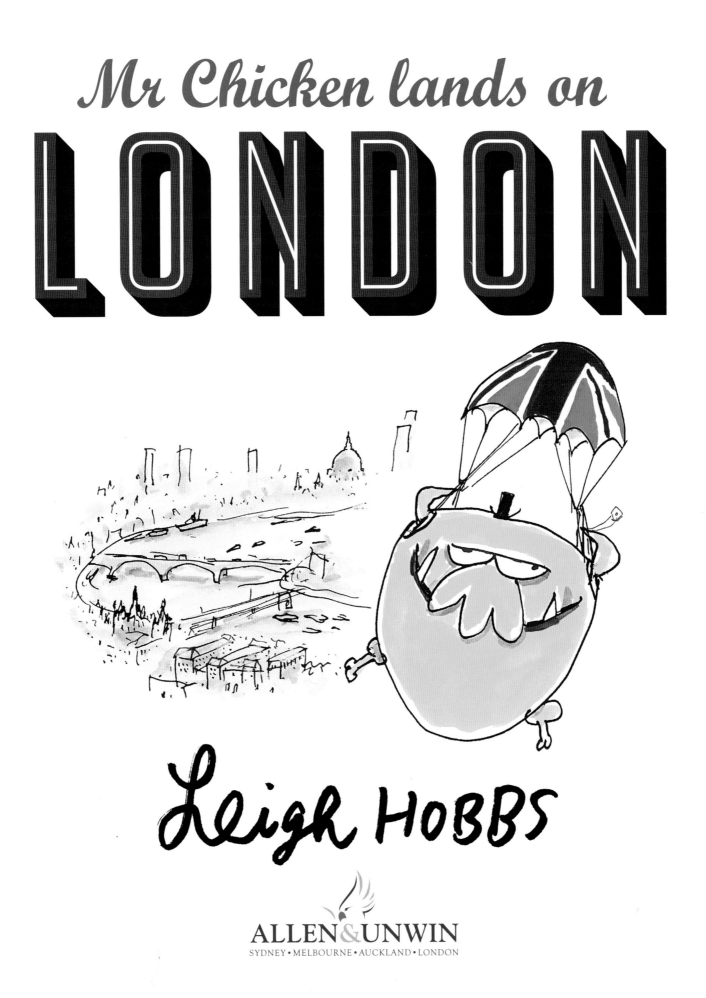

Leigh HOBBS

ALLEN&UNWIN

SYDNEY · MELBOURNE · AUCKLAND · LONDON

For three London companions,
John McKay, Susan Johnson and Jim Pavlidis

This paperback edition published in 2015

First published in Australia in 2014 by Allen & Unwin
First published in Great Britain in 2014 by Allen & Unwin

Allen & Unwin – Australia
83 Alexander Street, Crows Nest NSW 2065, Australia
Phone: (61 2) 8425 0100
Email: info@allenandunwin.com
Web: www.allenandunwin.com

A Cataloguing-in-Publication entry is available from
the National Library of Australia
www.trove.nla.gov.au
A catalogue record for this book is available from the British Library

ISBN 978 1 74336 522 9

Cover design by Leigh Hobbs and Sandra Nobes
Text design by Sandra Nobes
Set in 20 pt Cochin by Sandra Nobes
Colour reproduction by Splitting Image, Clayton, Victoria
This book was printed in November 2014 at 1010 Printing Limited
in Huizhou City, Guangdong Province, China

1 3 5 7 9 10 8 6 4 2

www.leighhobbs.com

The author wishes to thank Erica Wagner, Elise Jones and Sandra Nobes,
without whose help Mr Chicken would never have become airborne.

Mr Chicken couldn't wait another minute,
so he finished his breakfast, collected his camera and flew to London.

London was his favourite city in all the world.

After drifting over Regent Street,
he floated down through the clouds, past the Houses of Parliament,
before landing ever so gently right in the River Thames.

Luckily his camera was waterproof and the Savoy Hotel,
where he always stayed, was just around the corner.

'Good morning,' said Mr Chicken.
'I have a reservation.'

'Certainly, sir,' said Maurice,
the man at the desk. 'Welcome back.
Your favourite room is ready.'

When in London, Mr Chicken stayed in the River View Deluxe Room,
where he could look at London while enjoying breakfast in bed.

It was still early, so he ordered a full English breakfast
then planned his day and made a list.

Mr Chicken loved looking up facts and figures about his favourite city. He never got sick of learning new things.

Later, outside, a lost, teary tourist asked for directions. Mr Chicken was happy to help, for it made him feel like a real Londoner.

First on the list was
a visit to a special friend.
Whenever he was in town,
Mr Chicken called on
Her Majesty the Queen.

Of course, he always rang first,
so that Her Majesty had time
to do some extra baking.

'Oh, Mr Chicken, how lovely to hear from you!' the Queen said.
'Do pop in for morning tea.' And so he did.

At Buckingham Palace, Mr Chicken was on his best behaviour.
He took extra care not to break the furniture.

After morning tea, the Queen suggested stepping onto the balcony.
'The view is absolutely marvellous, Mr Chicken, as you well know.'
'I'd love to, Your Majesty,' said her gracious guest.

It was very nice indeed.
However, Mr Chicken had to
keep an eye on the time.

He had a lot
to do before lunch.

After the royal visit, Mr Chicken checked his list in St James's Park.

He'd seen the changing of the guard before, so he decided to climb up St Paul's Cathedral. Then he explored the Tower of London before crossing Tower Bridge.

By now Mr Chicken was getting behind in his schedule, as tourists kept wanting him to take their photo.

Even though Mr Chicken was a V.I.P. he liked to blend in.
He queued at bus stops and moved about on double-decker buses,
just as ordinary Londoners do.

If he was in a hurry, though, he drove the bus himself.

Of course, if Mr Chicken was in a *real* hurry he caught
the Underground. He enjoyed riding on the escalators,
especially if they took him to a favourite spot...

For instance, Trafalgar Square,
where Mr Chicken sometimes spied
on Lord Nelson standing atop his column.

Today, as there was room for two, and Lord Nelson didn't mind sharing, Mr Chicken joined him to take in the view. He didn't stay long, as his tummy told him it was nearly time for lunch.

Though he did manage to squeeze in a visit to the National Gallery.

'No touching, please, sir!' said a voice from behind.
'Pardon me,' said Mr Chicken.

With all that sightseeing, Mr Chicken had to keep his strength up. Luckily, his good manners and V.I.P. pass got him into very smart places for lunch.

'More tea, sir?' asked Walter the waiter.
'Make it cake, please,' answered the V.I.P.

Straight after lunch, he was back on a bus.
Mr Chicken wanted to see *everything*.

He even played 'I spy' on the London Eye.

In fact, Mr Chicken didn't stop until he found
a place to perch at Piccadilly Circus.

As usual, Mr Chicken had overdone his London sightseeing, and by late afternoon he'd become much too excited.

A short rest was needed back at the Savoy so he could freshen up.

In no time at all, Mr Chicken looked as good as ever and was ready for dinner.

'Vegetables, sir?'

'Yes, please,' answered Mr Chicken. 'Lots.'

A meal down in the crypt café of St Martin-in-the-Fields was a must
for Mr Chicken. He enjoyed it so much he was nearly late for the opera.

In the middle of the first act,
Mr Chicken remembered he had to be somewhere else.

By a quarter past nine…exactly.

He hurried down Whitehall
to the clock tower near
Parliament Square as
Big Ben struck nine.

At ten past nine,
Gerard the guard checked
Mr Chicken's V.I.P. pass.
'Yes, it's you all right, sir,'
he said, and waved him in.

Up, up, up climbed
Mr Chicken.

Tick! Tick! Tick! went the giant clock. At exactly a quarter past nine, Mr Chicken felt as if he was right inside the beating heart of London.

And that night,
at exactly a
quarter past nine,
Mr Chicken was.

Later, back at the hotel, sleep was impossible.

Not that it mattered very much, for Mr Chicken
didn't want to waste a minute.

So, as there was a full moon, he got up and went for a walk.

At midnight Mr Chicken listened to Big Ben strike twelve.
At last, he felt he had London all to himself.

In the morning it was time to leave, but not before a full English breakfast.
As always, Mr Chicken said goodbye to London from Waterloo Bridge.
And, as usual, he shed a tear.

Not a big one, of course,
for Mr Chicken knew he would soon be back.

EVERYTHING YOU NEED TO KNOW

LONDON. READ ALL ABOUT IT.

WATERLOO BRIDGE

London places to EAT

VERY IMPORTANT PERSON
V.I.P. CARD
The holder of this card is a very important person and is allowed in almost everywhere.

Name .... Mr Chicken.
Signature ...... MR Chicken

LONDON CHECKLIST.
Things to see and do this trip even though I have seen and done everything. (Well almost) by MR Chicken.

1. Full English breakfast.
2. Brisk walk down the Strand
3. Ring the Queen
4. Morning tea at Buckingham P. (I hope.)
5. ~~Stroll~~ Stroll through gardens.
6. Visit St Paul's Cathedral (check scones in restaurant)
7. Catch bus to Tower of L. and look at Tower Bridge.
8. Visit Trafalgar Square.
9. Go to National Gallery. Lunch either in the café or at my club. Maybe both if time.
10. Go for bus trip. The usual one.
11. Go on THE LONDON EYE (first time)
12. Rest later, at Piccadilly ~~Cir Circus~~ Circus.
13. Dinner before OPERA at St Martin-in-the-Fields ~~dinn~~ downstairs
14. OPERA - for an after-dinner rest
15. Walk down the Mall to Houses of Parliament. IMPORTANT TO BE THERE ON TIME.
16.

VIPs ...SEE LONDON WITH US!
LONDON on the move
LET US SHOW YOU!
500 STOPS
HOP ON and HOP OFF
V.I.P TOURS